JATAKA TALES—
ELEPHANT STORIES

THE GREEDY FORESTER*

THE BODHISATTVA ASSUMED MANY FORMS THROUGH MANY LIFE CYCLES. AND SO IT WAS THAT WHEN BRAHMADATTA REIGNED IN VARANASI, HE WAS BORN AN ELEPHANT IN A FOREST IN THE HIMALAYAS.

HAVE YOU SEEN THE NEW BABY?

NOT YET. LET'S GO. I HEAR THAT HE IS BEAUTIFUL.

IN A GROVE OF DEODAR TREES, THE PROUD MOTHER STOOD, HER NEWBORN BY HER SIDE.

HE'S WHITE ALL OVER AND SHINES LIKE MOLTEN SILVER.

HE LOOKS LIKE A FULL MOON LEANING ON A DARK CLOUD.

* BASED ON SEELAVA NAGARAJA JATAKA

1

THE ELEPHANT GREW UP IN THE FOREST, WITH OTHER LITTLE ELEPHANTS.

LET'S SHAKE THIS BRANCH TO FRIGHTEN THE MONKEY ON IT.

WATCH ME SUCK THIS SQUIRREL INTO MY TRUNK.

AS HE GREW OLDER, HE NOTICED THAT MOST OF HIS COMPANIONS WERE SELFISH, GREEDY, EVEN CRUEL.

AAAH! AAAH!

THE WHITE ELEPHANT DECIDED TO LEAVE THE HERD.

I DON'T BELONG HERE. I'D RATHER LIVE ALONE.

3

WHY, HE SEEMS HARMLESS! HE'S ONLY FOLLOWING ME, NOT CHASING ME AS I THOUGHT.

EVERY TIME HE MOVED, THE ELEPHANT FOLLOWED. EVERY TIME HE STOPPED THE ELEPHANT TOO STOPPED.

I'LL TURN ROUND AND STOP. LET'S SEE WHAT HE DOES.

TO HIS SURPRISE, THE ANIMAL SPOKE TO HIM

I HEARD YOU SCREAM. IS THERE ANYTHING I CAN DO FOR YOU?

WHAT A KIND, GENTLE VOICE! AND YET, SO DEEP AND POWERFUL!

I'VE LOST MY WAY. I WANT TO GO TO VARANASI.

COME HOME WITH ME. I'LL GUIDE YOU TO THE CITY.

LATER, AT THE ELEPHANT'S CAVE —

YOU ARE EXHAUSTED. WHY DON'T YOU REST HERE FOR A FEW DAYS?

I THINK I WILL.

THE ELEPHANT'S DAY BEGAN EARLY.

I LIKE TO WATCH THE DAY BREAK OVER THOSE HILLS AS I BATHE.

IN THE EVENING THEY WALKED TO A CLEARING IN THE FOREST.

LET US WATCH THE SUN GO DOWN. IT FILLS MY HEART WITH PEACE.

I ENVY YOU, YOUR PEACE OF MIND. WE MEN ARE RESTLESS CREATURES.

7

AT THE EDGE OF THE FOREST, HE DISMOUNTED.

THERE LIES THE ROAD TO VARANASI.

THANK YOU, MY FRIEND.

AND REMEMBER, YOU MUST KEEP MY HAUNTS A SECRET FROM ALL MEN.

A FEW DAYS LATER, THE FORESTER HAPPENED TO VISIT THE IVORY BAZAAR AT VARANASI.

WHAT BEAUTIFUL THINGS YOU CREATE!

THEY COULD BE EVEN MORE BEAUTIFUL, BUT GOOD TUSKS ARE HARD TO COME BY.

ARE THEY? WOULD THE TUSK OF A LIVING ELEPHANT BE GOOD ENOUGH?

IT'S THE BEST. BUT IT'S RARE AND COSTS MUCH MORE THAN THE TUSK OF A DEAD ONE.

GREED GOT THE BETTER OF THE FORESTER. HE WENT BACK TO THE FOREST.

WHAT IS THE MATTER? YOU LOOK UNHAPPY.

I AM UP TO MY NECK IN DEBT. A PIECE OF YOUR TUSK, CAN SAVE ME.

THE ELEPHANT SAT DOWN AND HELD HIS TRUNK OUT OBLIGINGLY.

I WILL GLADLY GIVE YOU BOTH MY TUSKS. BUT YOU WILL HAVE TO CUT THEM OFF.

I CAME PREPARED. I KNEW YOU WOULD NOT FAIL ME.

WHAT YOU HOLD ARE NO ORDINARY TUSKS. THEY ARE THE SOURCE OF ALL MY WISDOM.

BACK IN VARANASI, THE FORESTER RECEIVED A BIG SUM OF MONEY FOR THE TUSKS.

WHY, THERE IS MORE MONEY IN THIS THAN I THOUGHT! NOW I CAN BUY ALL THE SILKS AND JEWELS I WANT.

A MONTH LATER—

AFTER I BUY THESE THERE'LL BE NO MONEY LEFT. I SHOULD HAVE CUT CLOSER TO THE FLESH. WHAT A WASTE OF GOOD IVORY.

9

THAT NIGHT THE FORESTER COULD NOT SLEEP.

IF I CUT ANY MORE, THE ELEPHANT WILL SUFFER. BUT I MUST NOT BE SENTIMENTAL. I MUST GET HOLD OF THOSE PRECIOUS STUMPS OF TUSKS.

SO BACK HE WENT TO THE ELEPHANT. GREED HAD HARDENED HIS HEART.

YOUR TUSKS DID HELP TO CLEAR MY OLD DEBTS. BUT I NEED MORE MONEY IN ORDER TO LIVE.

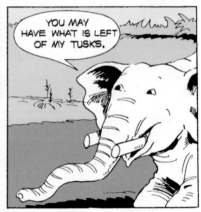

YOU MAY HAVE WHAT IS LEFT OF MY TUSKS.

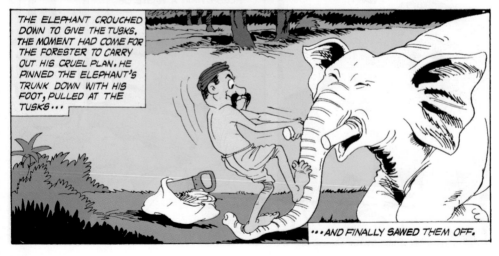

THE ELEPHANT CROUCHED DOWN TO GIVE THE TUSKS. THE MOMENT HAD COME FOR THE FORESTER TO CARRY OUT HIS CRUEL PLAN. HE PINNED THE ELEPHANT'S TRUNK DOWN WITH HIS FOOT, PULLED AT THE TUSKS...

...AND FINALLY SAWED THEM OFF.

AND HE WALKED AWAY, LEAVING THE ELEPHANT TORN AND TREMBLING. NOT A WORD OF REPROACH ESCAPED THE ELEPHANT'S LIPS.

SUDDENLY THE FORESTER FELT THE GROUND HEAVE UNDER HIS FEET. THE EARTH SPLIT OPEN AND A FIRE RAGED.

HELP! HELP!

THE FORESTER REALISED THAT HE WAS BEING PUN — ISHED FOR HIS GREED; BUT IT WAS TOO LATE.

AS THE FLAMES CONSUMED HIM, A VOICE WAS HEARD —

AN UNGRATE — FUL MAN IS NEVER SATISFIED — NOT EVEN IF HE IS GIVEN THE WHOLE WORLD.

AS FOR THE WISE ELEPHANT, HE LIVED THE REST OF HIS LIFE IN THE PEACE AND QUIET OF THE HIMALAYAS.

THE BRAVE QUAIL*

IN A FOREST NEAR VARANASI, THERE ONCE LIVED SOME QUAILS. THE SHADY GROVE IN WHICH THEY NESTED WAS ALSO THE FAVOURITE GRAZING GROUND OF A HERD OF ELEPHANTS. A WISE AND JUST ELEPHANT, THE BODHISATTVA, WAS THE LEADER OF THAT HERD.

ONE DAY, ONE OF THE QUAILS LAID SOME EGGS.

I HOPE MY EGGS WILL BE SAFE TILL THEY ARE HATCHED.

YOU WILL HAVE TO KEEP CAREFUL WATCH. YOU KNOW HOW CARELESS THE ELEPHANTS ARE.

SOON THE FLEDGLINGS WERE HATCHED. ONE DAY—

LOOK! THE ELEPHANTS ARE MAKING FOR OUR GROVE!

WHAT SHALL I DO? I CAN ONLY FALL AT THEIR FEET AND BEG FOR PROTECTION.

* BASED ON LATUKIKA JATAKA

AS THE LEADER CAME CLOSE —

O MIGHTY ELEPHANT, MY LITTLE ONES ARE IN DANGER. IF YOUR HERD ENTERS THIS GROVE, THEY WILL BE TRAMPLED TO DEATH.

DO NOT FEAR. YOUR FLEDGLINGS WILL NOT BE HARMED.

THE ELEPHANT STOOD OVER THE NEST WHILE HIS HERD GRAZED. WHEN THEY HAD HAD THEIR FILL —

THERE IS A ROGUE-ELEPHANT, A WILD AND DANGEROUS ANIMAL, WHO MIGHT SOON BE COMING THIS WAY.

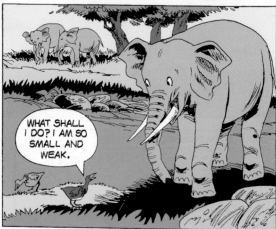

WHAT SHALL I DO? I AM SO SMALL AND WEAK.

YOU MUST APPEAL TO HIM FOR MERCY AND HOPE FOR THE BEST.

SOON AFTER THE ELEPHANTS HAD GONE —

THE ROGUE-ELEPHANT!

HE LOOKS FIERCE!

THE MOTHER QUAIL WASTED NO TIME. SHE WAS AT HIS FEET, HER HEAD LOWERED IN SALUTE.

HOW DARE YOU COME IN MY WAY?

O POWERFUL ONE, I BEG OF YOU, SPARE MY YOUNG ONES!

THE ELEPHANT LASHED AT THE NEST.

THERE! THAT IS THE END OF YOUR SILLY BROOD.

AS THE QUAIL WEPT OVER THE REMAINS OF HER DEAD CHILDREN—

I WILL SOON SHOW YOU HOW STRONG I AM!

GRIEF HAD MADE HER BOLD AND SET HER THINKING HARD. SHE WENT TO A CROW AND TOLD HIM HER SAD TALE.

YOU MUST SPOT THIS **ROGUE-ELEPHANT** AND PECK OUT BOTH HIS EYES.

DEPEND ON ME. SUCH WICKEDNESS SHOULD NOT GO UNPUNISHED.

HAVING GOT THE CROW ON HER SIDE, THE QUAIL WENT TO AN ANT.

MY LITTLE FRIEND, I NEED YOUR HELP.

I HEARD ABOUT YOUR BABIES. I AM DEEPLY GRIEVED.

THAT IS WHY I AM HERE. WE MUST TEACH THE CRUEL ELEPHANT A LESSON.

HOW CAN I HELP?

MY FRIEND THE CROW WILL PECK OUT HIS EYES. AFTER THAT YOU MUST LAY YOUR EGGS IN THE EMPTY SOCKETS.

A GOOD IDEA! WHEN THEY HATCH, MY LITTLE ONES WILL BEGIN TO BITE.

THE QUAIL THEN WENT TO THE FROG.

DEAR FRIEND, LEAVE EVERYTHING AND COME OUT!

THE FROG ROSE TO THE SURFACE AND CROAKED.

WHAT IS THE MATTER?

ALL MY YOUNG ONES WERE CRUELLY KILLED BY A SPITEFUL ELEPHANT.

I AM TRYING TO GET MY FRIENDS TO HELP ME PUNISH HIM.

YOU CAN COUNT ON ME.

AS THEY WENT ALONG, THE QUAIL UNFOLDED HER PLANS.

···WHEN THE ANTS HATCH, THE ROGUE-ELEPHANT WILL BE BADLY STUNG. HE WILL RUN BLINDLY, LOOKING FOR WATER TO EASE HIS PAIN. THIS IS WHAT I WANT YOU TO DO···

A LITTLE LATER, THE CROW DARTED AT THE ELEPHANT...

... PLUCKED HIS EYES OUT. AND FLEW AWAY.

A-A-AH!

THEN, THE ANT LAID HER EGGS IN HIS BLIND EYES.

A-A-AH!
MY EYES ARE
ON FIRE. WATER!
I NEED WATER!

JUST THEN THE FROG CROAKED FROM A STEEP PRECIPICE CLOSE BY.

AS THE ELEPHANT GOT TO THE EDGE OF THE PRECIPICE...

...THE FROG LEAPT ONTO A NARROW LEDGE BELOW AND CROAKED WITH ALL HIS MIGHT.

THE ROYAL ELEPHANT*

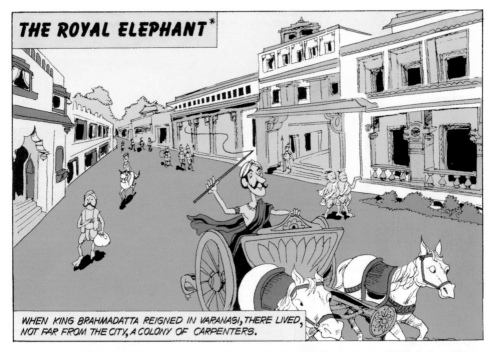

WHEN KING BRAHMADATTA REIGNED IN VARANASI, THERE LIVED, NOT FAR FROM THE CITY, A COLONY OF CARPENTERS.

EVERY DAY THEY WOULD SAIL DOWN THE RIVER AND ENTER A DENSE FOREST TO FELL TREES FOR TIMBER.

THUS THEY MOVED FROM FOREST TO VILLAGE AND BACK AGAIN. WORK WAS PLENTIFUL.

WE NEVER SEEM TO HAVE ENOUGH WOOD!

I NEVER SEEM TO HAVE ENOUGH TIME.

*BASED ON ALEENACHITTA JATAKA

ONE DAY, AS THEY SAT DOWN TO THEIR MIDDAY MEAL, THEY SAW AN ELEPHANT.

HE'S COMING TOWARDS US.

HE IS LIMPING AND SEEMS TO BE IN GREAT PAIN.

THE ELEPHANT CAME UP TO THE CARPENTERS AND HELD OUT A FOOT.

I STEPPED ON SOMETHING—I THINK IT'S A SPLINTER.

YOU ARE RIGHT. IT HAS ENTERED QUITE DEEP INTO THE FLESH.

THEY REMOVED THE SPLINTER, BATHED AND DRESSED THE WOUND AND NURSED THE FOOT BACK TO HEALTH.

YOU HAVE BEEN VERY KIND TO ME. I WOULD LIKE TO COME HERE EVERY DAY AND HELP YOU.

THE ELEPHANT SERVED THEM WELL FOR A NUMBER OF YEARS. ONE DAY—

LOOK! OUR FRIEND HAS BROUGHT A YOUNG ONE WITH HIM TODAY.

WHAT A BEAUTIFUL WHITE ANIMAL!

I AM NO LONGER AS ACTIVE AS I USED TO BE. I HAVE BROUGHT MY SON TO TAKE MY PLACE.

I WILL TRY MY BEST TO PLEASE YOU IN EVERY WAY.

THE YOUNG ELEPHANT WORKED HARD. HE HELPED TO LOAD AND UNLOAD TIMBER.

HE FETCHED AND CARRIED TOOLS...

...AND TRANSPORTED LOGS.

MORE, HE BROUGHT JOY AND LAUGHTER INTO THE CARPENTERS' LIVES FOR HE KEPT THEIR CHILDREN AMUSED.

OOOH! WHAT A LOVELY SWING!

ONE DAY, QUITE BY ACCIDENT, THE RAIN WASHED SOME OF HIS DROPPINGS INTO THE RIVER. LATER, DOWNSTREAM, WHERE THE ROYAL ELEPHANTS BATHED —

OUR ELEPHANTS ARE REFUSING TO GET INTO THE WATER.

LET US REPORT THE MATTER TO THE KING.

THE TRAINER GUESSED THE TRUTH.

THE WATER CONTAINS THE DROPPINGS OF A NOBLE ANIMAL. HE MUST LIVE UP-STREAM SOME-WHERE.

WHEN THE TRAINER REPORT-ED THE MATTER TO THE KING —

SCOUR THE COUNTRYSIDE. IF THERE IS SUCH AN ANIMAL HE SHOULD ADORN THE ROYAL STABLES.

THE KING HIMSELF SET OUT WITH A BAND OF TRUSTED MEN.

WITHIN MINUTES THEY TRACED THE ELEPHANT.

THAT MUST BE THE ANIMAL WE ARE LOOKING FOR. HOW NOBLY HE BEARS HIMSELF!

SOON —

THE KING!

DO YOU THINK HE WANTS US TO WORK IN THE PALACE?

IF HE DID, HE WOULD SEND FOR US, NOT COME HERE HIMSELF.

WHEN THE KING AND HIS PARTY DREW NEARER —

YOUR MAJESTY, WE ARE HONOURED. HOW CAN WE BE OF SERVICE TO YOU?

WE WOULD LIKE THIS ELEPHANT FOR OUR ROYAL STABLES.

THE ELEPHANT SEIZED THE OPPORTUNITY TO HELP HIS FRIENDS.

THESE MEN HAVE BEEN VERY KIND TO ME. I AM GREATLY INDEBTED TO THEM.

THE KING TURNED TO HIS MEN.

PAY THEM A HUNDRED THOUSAND PIECES OF GOLD FOR HIS TAIL, THE SAME FOR HIS TRUNK AND FOR EACH OF HIS FOUR FEET.

THE ELEPHANT WAS NOT SATISFIED.

YOU MUST NOT THINK ME GREEDY, YOUR MAJESTY. THEY NEED CLOTHES. AND THE CHILDREN TOO MUST BE PROVIDED FOR.

WE ADMIRE YOUR LOYALTY. WE SHALL MORE THAN SATISFY YOU.

UPON RECEIVING THIS ASSURANCE THE ELEPHANT AGREED TO GO WITH THE KING. IT WAS A SAD LEAVE-TAKING.

A KING'S COMMAND MUST BE OBEYED. YOU ARE GOOD CHILDREN AND WILL UNDERSTAND.

WHO WILL PLAY WITH US?

AND THE ELEPHANT LEFT FOR VARANASI WITH THE KING AND HIS MEN.

THE CITY WORE A FESTIVE AIR. THE ELEPHANT, REGALLY CAPARISONED, WAS LED TO HIS GAILY DECORATED STABLE.

THE NOBLES AND MINISTERS LOOKED ON IN ADMIRATION.

HE IS THE MOST MAJESTIC ANIMAL I HAVE EVER SEEN.

MARK MY WORDS! HE WILL PROVE HIS WORTH IN TIMES OF WAR.

THE KING MADE OVER HALF HIS KINGDOM TO THE ELEPHANT.

YOU ARE A BROTHER TO ME AND A COMPANION FOR LIFE.

THE ELEPHANT BECAME DEEPLY ATTACHED TO THE KING AND FOLLOWED HIM EVERYWHERE.

MY LORD, HE REFUSES TO TOUCH HIS FOOD TILL YOU HAVE FIRST FED HIM A MORSEL.

A FEW MONTHS LATER, THE QUEEN WAS EXPECTING A BABY.

THE ELEPHANT HAS BROUGHT US GREAT GOOD FORTUNE. MY POWER AS A MONARCH IS NOW UNCHALLENGED.

I FEEL OUR CHILD IS DESTINED FOR GREAT THINGS.

BUT THEIR JOY WAS SHORT-LIVED. THE KING FELL SERIOUSLY ILL. AS HE LAY DYING—

MY ELEPHANT WILL BE BROKEN-HEARTED.

OUR CHILD WILL NEVER KNOW A FATHER!

WHEN THE KING DIED—

WE MUST KEEP THE SAD NEWS FROM THE ELEPHANT.

I WONDER HOW LONG IT WILL BE BEFORE HE FINDS OUT!

MEANWHILE, THE KING OF KOSALA WAS MARCHING TOWARDS VARANASI.

THE KING IS DEAD, AND CONFUSION REIGNS.

THERE WERE HURRIED CONSULTATIONS AT VARANASI.

WE SHOULD ASK THEM TO SUSPEND FIGHTING FOR A WEEK.

HOW WILL THAT HELP?

ACCORDING TO THE ASTROLOGERS, THE QUEEN WILL GIVE BIRTH TO HER CHILD WITHIN A WEEK. IF IT IS A SON, WE WILL FIGHT. IF NOT, WE WILL SURRENDER.

THE KING OF KOSALA ACCEDED TO THEIR REQUEST.

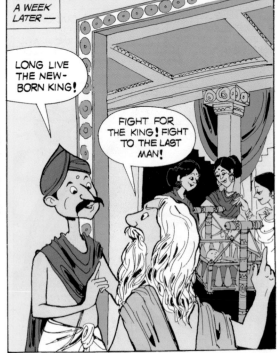

A WEEK LATER —

LONG LIVE THE NEW-BORN KING!

FIGHT FOR THE KING! FIGHT TO THE LAST MAN!

29

THE ELEPHANT KNELT TO RECEIVE THE QUEEN'S BLESSING.

I SHALL TALK NO MORE OF DEATH. YOUR SON SHALL RULE.

WE NOW HAVE SOMETHING TO LIVE FOR.

AS THE KEEPER OF THE ROYAL STABLES GOT HIM READY FOR THE BATTLE...

... THE KING'S MEN FELT THEIR HOPES RISE.

GET THE TROOPS OUT! LET NO MAN DAWDLE!

AND THEN THE ELEPHANT CHARGED FORWARD, THE SKIES RESOUNDING WITH HIS MIGHTY TRUMPETING.

PUT COURAGE IN YOUR HEARTS AND STRENGTH IN YOUR ARMS!

FOLLOW OUR LEADER. HE IS DIVINELY INSPIRED!

THE KOSALA ARMIES WERE ROUTED. THE BATTLE WON. THE ELEPHANT STOOD BEFORE THE QUEEN, HIS PROUD HEAD BOWED BEFORE HIS INFANT MASTER.

MY GRIEF IS GREAT FOR YOUR DEAD FATHER. BUT I LIVE FOR YOU AND FOR THE GREAT DESTINY THAT AWAITS YOU, MY PRINCE.

AND THE BODHISATTVA (FOR THE CHILD WAS NONE OTHER THAN HE) GREW UP TO INHERIT A KING-DOM WHICH HE RULED WISELY AND WELL.

The route to your roots

MONKEY STORIES

Monkeys frolic through these pages, imparting lessons in leadership and common sense. Murderous crocodiles, powerful kings and fearsome ogres are easily outwitted by these winsome creatures. All they seem to need is careful thought and a lot of courage. But be warned: do not let monkeys loose in your garden or you may well lose sight of their virtues!

Script
Meena Talim

Illustrations
Jeffrey Fowler

Editor
Anant Pai

★ THE MONKEY KING'S SACRIFICE

FRIENDS! WE HAVE BEEN LIVING HAPPILY ON THIS MANGO TREE FOR YEARS.

WHY MASTER?

BUT I ANTICIPATE TROUBLE, SOON.

MEN HAVE COME TO LIVE NEAR OUR FOREST. THEY HAVE NEVER TASTED THE MANGO FRUIT.

★ BASED ON MAHA KAPI JATAKA

1

ONCE THEY DO, IT WILL BE DANGEROUS FOR US.

OH DEAR! WHAT SHALL WE DO?

MAKE SURE THAT NOT A SINGLE FRUIT FALLS INTO THE RIVER.

PLUCK EACH AND EVERY BUD FROM THE BRANCHES THAT SPREAD OUT OVER THE RIVER.

BUT IN SPITE OF ALL THIS CARE, A JUICY RIPE MANGO FELL INTO THE RIVER...

SPLAT

... AND GOT CAUGHT IN A FISHERMAN'S NET.

THEY WERE LET IN.

OH MASTER, THIS FRUIT WAS AMONG THE FISH I CAUGHT.

HM-M!

SEND FOR THE FORESTER. HE WILL TELL US WHAT FRUIT IT IS.

THAT'S THE RARE MANGO, SIR.

IS IT POISONOUS? NOT AT ALL, SIR. IN FACT IT IS VERY TASTY.

SO THE KING SUNK HIS TEETH INTO IT.

HM-M-M! DELICIOUS.

IT SMELLS GOOD, TOO!

4

NEXT MORNING —

TELL ME FORESTER, WHERE DOES THIS MANGO FRUIT GROW.

THERE IS A MAN-GO GROVE, JUST A LITTLE UPSTREAM, SIR.

MINISTER, MAKE THE NECESSARY ARRANGEMENTS. WE ARE LEAVING FOR THAT GROVE.

YES, SIR.

SOON THEY WERE OFF.

I HOPE YOU HAVE BROUGHT SOME ARCHERS ALONG.

I HAVE, SIR.

WHEN THEY REACHED THE SPOT —

TELL EVERYONE TO EAT AS MUCH AS THEY CAN.

MINISTER, WE WILL STAY HERE FOR A DAY OR TWO.

I WILL MAKE THE ARRANGE-MENTS, SIR.

AS NIGHT FELL, THE MONKEYS BEGAN MOVING ABOUT.

MINISTER, WHAT WAS THAT?

JUST MONKEYS SIR, SCAMPERING AMONG THE BRANCHES.

WHEN IT'S MORNING, TELL THE ARCHERS TO SHOOT EVERY SINGLE MONKEY.

I SHALL, SIR.

THE NEXT MORNING—

TODAY ALONG WITH THE MANGOES WE SHALL EAT MONKEY'S FLESH.

OH MASTER, WE'RE TRAPPED.

WHAT ARE WE TO DO NOW?

EYOW

DON'T PANIC. I'LL FIND A WAY OUT.

6

THEY MANAGED TO GET TO A TREE NEAR THE RIVER.

NOW ALL OF YOU DO AS I TELL YOU.

HE GOT HOLD OF A THICK LONG CREEPER. HE TIED ONE END OF IT TO A BRANCH AND THE OTHER TO HIS WAIST.

NOW I WILL SWING OVER THE RIVER TO THAT FIG TREE ON THE OPPOSITE BANK. ONE BY ONE YOU CAN COME ACROSS TO THE OTHER SIDE.

OH NO! THE VINE IS TOO SHORT.

I WILL TRY TO GET HOLD OF THIS BRANCH AND BRIDGE THE GAP.

7

LOOK AT THAT MONKEY KING. HOW HE MUST LOVE HIS SUBJECTS.

THE MONKEYS BEGAN CROSSING.

WHAT ARE YOU WAITING FOR? CROSS OVER MY BACK.

BUT, MASTER, HOW CAN I...

THIS IS NO TIME TO THINK ABOUT SUCH THINGS. CROSS QUICKLY.

YOU ARE VERY KIND, MASTER.

ALL THE MONKEYS CROSSED OVER IN THIS MANNER. THE LAST ONE WAS A WICKED MONKEY WHO HAD NEVER LIKED HIS KING.

HERE IS MY CHANCE TO TAKE REVENGE.

I SHALL JUMP ACROSS AND PUSH HIM DOWN.

COME ON. PLEASE HURRY.

★THE STUPID CROCODILE AND THE MONKEY

★ BASED ON VANARINDA JATAKA

THE NEXT DAY AS USUAL THE MONKEY SET OUT FOR THE ISLAND.

I'M HUNGRY!

SO AM I! HEE! HEE!

WHEN HE HAD EATEN TO HIS STOMACH'S CONTENT—

HEY! THAT'S STRANGE! THAT ROCK LOOKS BIGGER TODAY.

THE RIVER HAS NOT GONE DRY FOR IT TO LOOK BIGGER.

I'M SURE IT IS THAT STUPID CROCODILE, UP TO HIS TRICKS AGAIN. I WON'T JUMP TILL I'M SURE.

LET ME SEE IF THIS IDEA WORKS.

HELLO ROCK! HOW ARE YOU TODAY, MY FRIEND?

THE MONKEY CALLED OVER AND OVER AGAIN.

WHY AREN'T YOU SPEAKING TO ME TODAY ROCK? HAVE I ANNOYED YOU?

IT LOOKS AS IF THIS ROCK USED TO TALK TO HIM. I'D BETTER REPLY.

?

14

15

AS THE MONKEY HAD EXPECTED, THE MOMENT THE CROCODILE OPENED HIS MOUTH WIDE, HIS EYES CLOSED.

NOW'S MY CHANCE. I'LL JUMP ON HIM AND ONTO THE BANK. I'LL HAVE TO BE QUICK.

TAKE THAT!

THUD

WHAT WAS THAT?

WHAT ARE YOU DOING OVER THERE? YOU PROMISED YOU WOULD JUMP INTO MY MOUTH.

DID YOU REALLY BELIEVE I'D DO A STUPID THING LIKE THAT?

GRR! WAIT TILL I GET MY TEETH INTO YOU.

YOU NEVER WILL, CROCODILE. YOU MAY BE BIG AND STRONG BUT YOU ARE STUPID.

16

★THE DEMON OUTWITTED

LONG AGO A BAND OF MONKEYS CAME AND SETTLED ON THE OUTSKIRTS OF A FOREST.

THE LEADER WHO KNEW THE PLACE WELL, CALLED A MEETING.

ATTENTION, ALL OF YOU! I HAVE SOMETHING IMPORTANT TO SAY.

YOU WILL HAVE TO BE CAREFUL ABOUT TWO THINGS IN THIS FOREST.

THERE ARE CERTAIN POISONOUS TREES WITH VERY TEMPTING FRUIT AND ONE OF THE LAKES IS HAUNTED BY A DEMON.

★ BASED ON NALAPANA JATAKA

YOU MUST NOT DRINK WATER OR EAT ANY FRUIT WITHOUT ASKING ME.

ONE DAY WHILE SEARCHING FOR FIREWOOD, THE MONKEYS WANDERED DEEP INTO THE FOREST.

MOTHER, I'M THIRSTY.

AH! THERE IS A LAKE CLOSE BY.

WAIT! DON'T GO NEAR THE WATER.

DON'T YOU REMEMBER OUR LEADER'S WARNING?

OH DEAR! I'D COMPLETELY FORGOTTEN. THANK YOU FOR REMINDING ME.

ALL RIGHT! LET US WAIT TILL OUR LEADER COMES.

19

22

...THE WATER GUSHED OUT IN A THICK STREAM.

SPLAT

WATER! DELICIOUS WATER! AND ALL FOR US.

FULL OF RAGE, THE OUTWITTED DEMON STOMPED BACK INTO THE LAKE.

GRRRR!

HA HA HA HO HO HEE HO HAHA

AND THE MONKEYS THEIR THIRST WELL QUENCHED, RETURNED HOME.

★ BASED ON SUMSUMARA JATAKA

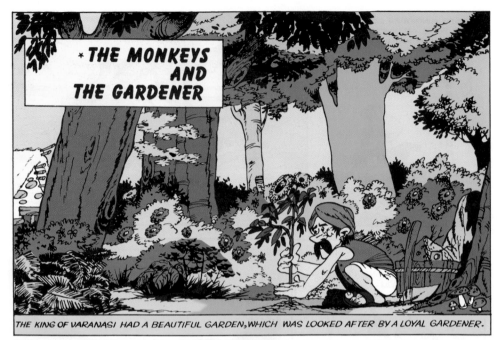

THE KING OF VARANASI HAD A BEAUTIFUL GARDEN, WHICH WAS LOOKED AFTER BY A LOYAL GARDENER.

ONE NIGHT —

HELLO FRIEND. THE FESTIVAL IN TOWN BEGINS TOMORROW.

I KNOW!

THERE'S GOING TO BE PLENTY OF FUN.

HOW I WISH I COULD COME!

WHAT! AREN'T YOU COMING?

IF I DO, WHO WILL WATER THE GARDEN?

★ BASED ON ARMADUSAKA JATAKA

28

29

30

MEANWHILE IN TOWN —

I WONDER HOW MY MONKEY FRIENDS ARE GETTING ALONG WITH THEIR TASK?

TWO DAYS LATER THE GARDENER RETURNED HOME.

WHAT HAVE YOU DONE?

WE WATERED EACH PLANT ACCORDING TO THE NEEDS OF ITS ROOTS

THAT'S RIGHT. WE DID.

WHATEVER, SHALL I DO NOW? WHAT SHALL I TELL THE KING?

THAT'S WHAT COMES OF DEPENDING ON A FOOL. HE MAY MEAN WELL BUT WILL END UP DOING MORE HARM THAN ANYTHING ELSE.

DEER STORIES

The route to your roots

DEER STORIES

Deer, in the Jataka tales, are often gentle bodhisattvas or Buddhas-to-be. They are noble, selfless, wise and virtuous. As models of right thinking and right living, they strongly advise a life of non-violence and peace for ultimate happiness. Even if greed leads them astray, they are soon guided back to the correct path.

Script
The Editorial Team

Illustrations
Jeffrey Fowler

Editor
Anant Pai

TRUE FRIENDSHIP

IN A THICKET NEAR A LAKE, LIVED THREE FRIENDS, A TORTOISE, A WOODPECKER AND AN *ANTELOPE.

ONE DAY A HUNTER CAME THAT WAY.

AH! FOOTPRINTS! I'LL SET THE TRAP RIGHT HERE.

HE IS BOUND TO PASS THIS WAY TO DRINK WATER.

I'LL COME BACK FOR HIM TOMORROW.

AT DAWN —

IT'S GOOD TO BE ALIVE. I MUST HAVE A DRINK.

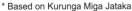

* Based on Kurunga Miga Jataka

A deer-like animal, which has horns instead of antlers

1

HELP!!

THE TORTOISE AND THE WOODPECKER HEARD HIS CRIES AND RUSHED TO HIM.

I'LL TELL YOU WHAT — YOU HAVE STRONG TEETH. YOU FREE HIM WHILE I KEEP THE HUNTER AWAY.

WHEN HE COMES OUT OF HIS HUT, I'LL GIVE HIM A GOOD PECKING.

THE TORTOISE WAS AS SLOW AS A TORTOISE COULD BE.

WILL YOU PLEASE HURRY.

2

MEANWHILE THE HUNTER TOO HAD HEARD THE ANTELOPE'S SHOUTS FOR HELP AND HAD RUSHED OUT.

SLAM

AH...AH, HE'S CAUGHT.

THE WOOD-PECKER SPIED HIM.

ZOOM

EYOOW

CRACK

SCREEEEEEEECH!!

I'D BETTER GET INDOORS.

PUFF PANT PUFF

I'VE GOT IT, I'LL TRY TO GO OUT BY THE BACK DOOR.

BUT—

I BET HE WILL TRY TO GET OUT FROM THE BACK DOOR.

3

LEAVING HIM THERE THE WOODPECKER FLEW BACK TO HIS FRIENDS.

IT WAS NOW THE ANTELOPE'S TURN TO SAVE HIS FRIEND.

IF HE SEES ME, HE WILL CHASE ME, AND MY FRIEND CAN ESCAPE.

THE ANTELOPE SHOWED HIMSELF.

THERE GOES MY ANTELOPE.

THE HUNTER DROPPED HIS SACK AND RAN AFTER THE ANTELOPE.

I'LL LEAD HIM INTO MY FAVOURITE OLD CAVE.

ONCE HE IS IN HE WILL NOT KNOW HOW TO GET OUT.

WHAT A FOOL! HE'LL BE TRAPPED IN THE CAVE. HE'S DONE FOR.

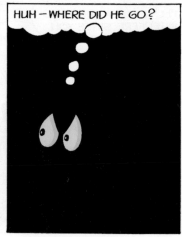

HUH — WHERE DID HE GO?

*RURU, THE GOLDEN DEER

MAHADHANAKA WAS THE SON OF A RICH MERCHANT OF VARANASI. HIS FATHER, INSTEAD OF SENDING HIM TO SCHOOL, SPOILT HIM WITH ALL THE PLEASURES OF THE WORLD.

ENJOY YOURSELF, MY SON! I CAN GIVE YOU EVERYTHING.

I KNOW, FATHER!

WHEN HE CAME OF AGE, MAHADHANAKA WAS MARRIED TO A BEAUTIFUL GIRL.

YOUR MOTHER HAS COOKED THIS FOR YOU, MY LORD.

HM...M...M, IT SMELLS DELICIOUS!

SOON HIS PARENTS DIED AND HE WAS LEFT ALONE.

ALAS! WHO WILL LOOK AFTER ME NOW?

HIS FRIENDS WERE AFTER HIS MONEY.

COME ON MAHADHANAKA, CHEER UP. LET US HAVE A GAME OF DICE AND SOME WINE TO WARM US UP.

YES, THAT'S A GOOD IDEA.

* Based on Ruru Jataka

MAHADHANAKA HAD NEVER HANDLED MONEY BEFORE, SO HE DID NOT KNOW HOW TO USE IT.

USE THE MOST EXPENSIVE CLOTH YOU HAVE, FOR OUR CLOTHES.

I CERTAINLY WILL, SIR.

LET US HAVE SOME MORE LIQUOR AND PLAY ANOTHER ROUND OF CARDS.

ONE DAY— WHAT! NO MONEY! IF I DON'T DO SOMETHING I'LL SOON HAVE NO FRIENDS EITHER.

YES, THAT'S IT. I'LL BORROW SOME MONEY AND PAY IT BACK LATER.

HE WENT FROM ONE MONEY-LENDER TO ANOTHER AND PROMISED THEM THE SAME THING.

I'LL RETURN YOUR MONEY AS SOON AS I BECOME RICH AGAIN.

9

MONTHS PASSED. WHEN MAHADHANAKA SHOWED NO SIGN OF RETURNING THE MONEY—

YOU HAD BETTER PAY UP SOON, MAHADHANAKA, OR ELSE...

HAVE PATIENCE. I WILL.

BUT HE KNEW HE WOULD NEVER BE ABLE TO REPAY THE MONEY. AT LAST—

I WOULD RATHER DIE THAN FACE THE MONEY-LENDERS.

THEN ONE DAY MAHADHANAKA LED ALL HIS CREDITORS TO THE BANK OF A RIVER.

WHERE ARE YOU LEADING US?

I HAVE SOME TREASURE HIDDEN IN THE RIVER BED. I WILL RETURN ALL THAT I HAVE BORROWED FROM YOU.

NOW IS MY CHANCE TO SLIP AWAY, AND DROWN MYSELF. THAT WILL BE THE END TO ALL MY SORROWS.

SPLASH!

HELP! GLUB! GASP! HELP!

NOT VERY FAR AWAY, ON THE OPPOSITE BANK, LIVED RURU, A GOLDEN DEER.

SOMEBODY'S DROWNING. I MUST SAVE HIM.

HELP! HELP!!

HO! MAN. I WILL SAVE YOUR LIFE. HOLD ON.

GASP!!

?

SLOWLY NOW.

GLUB!

HOW DO YOU FEEL?

MUCH BETTER. THANK YOU.

BEFORE PARTING, PROMISE ME YOU WILL TELL NO ONE ABOUT ME AND WHERE I LIVE.

I PROMISE, FRIEND.

THAT NIGHT KHEMA, THE QUEEN OF VARANASI, HAD A DREAM.

SHE WOKE UP THE KING.

WHAT IS IT, MY QUEEN?

I DREAMT THAT A GOLDEN DEER PREACHED DHARMA TO ME. IF SUCH A DEER EXISTS, I WOULD LIKE TO HEAR ITS DISCOURSE.

IF THERE IS SUCH AN ANIMAL, YOU WILL.

THE KING SENT FOR HIS COUNCILLORS.

ARE THERE SUCH ANIMALS AS GOLDEN DEER?

YES, YOUR MAJESTY. THERE ARE.

I SHALL GIVE A REWARD TO THE MAN WHO CAN FIND ONE FOR ME.

THE REWARD WAS A SACK OF GOLD COINS PLACED IN A GOLD POT ON AN ELEPHANT'S BACK.

5

A TOWN CRIER WAS SENT TO TELL THE PEOPLE OF THE REWARD.

JUST THEN MAHADHANAKA STROLLED BY.

WHAT DID YOU SAY, MY FRIEND?

THE KING IS OFFERING A LARGE REWARD TO ANY MAN WHO CAN TELL HIM OF THE WHEREABOUTS OF A GOLDEN DEER.

HMMMM, I SHALL SOON BE RICH AGAIN.

TAKE ME TO THE KING.

SO HE WENT WITH THE COURTIER TO THE PALACE.

YOUR MAJESTY, THIS MAN SAYS HE KNOWS WHERE A GOLDEN DEER MAY BE FOUND.

HMMM!

IS THAT SO? WHEN CAN YOU LEAD US TO HIM.

AT THE BREAK OF DAWN, YOUR MAJESTY.

AT DAWN—

I HOPE YOU KNOW THE WAY.

THERE, YOUR MAJESTY, IN THAT GROVE OF MANGO AND SAL TREES, LIVES THE GOLDEN DEER YOU WANT.

SURROUND THE GROVE.

I'LL STAND A LITTLE WAY OFF AND SEE WHAT HAPPENS.

TIP TOE

WHEN THE DEER HEARD THE NOISE OF THE BEATERS —

CLANG THUMP

THAT'S A HUNTING PARTY, I'M SURE. HOW DID THEY FIND THIS GROVE?

14

PUT DOWN YOUR BOW, O KING. I'VE SOMETHING TO ASK YOU.

THE KING WAS ASTONISHED TO HEAR RURU'S VOICE.

I PROMISE I WON'T SHOOT. COME OUT OF YOUR HIDING PLACE.

WHAT IS IT YOU WANT TO KNOW?

YOUR MAJESTY, WHO TOLD YOU ABOUT ME AND WHERE I LIVE?

HE DID.

I THOUGHT AS MUCH. IT WOULD HAVE BEEN BETTER TO SAVE A LOG OF WOOD THAN A MAN LIKE HIM.

? WHAT DO YOU MEAN BY THAT?

YOUR MAJESTY, I ONCE SAVED THIS MAN FROM DROWNING, AND THIS IS HOW HE HAS REPAID ME.

IS THAT SO? HE SHALL BE HANGED FOR IT.

NO, DON'T DO THAT. I DON'T WANT HIM TO DIE BECAUSE OF ME.

YOU ARE LUCKY. BUT FOR HIM I WOULD HAVE HAD YOU HANGED. NOW GO AWAY.

THE KING THEN TURNED TO RURU.

ASK FOR ANYTHING, AND I'LL GRANT IT TO YOU.

YOUR MAJESTY, FROM NOW ON, LET NO ANIMAL OR BIRD BE HARMED BY ANYONE IN YOUR KINGDOM.

THEN THE KING IMMEDIATELY SENT AROUND A PROCLAMATION.

NO LIVING CREATURE BIG OR SMALL SHALL HENCEFORTH BE HARMED. SHOULD ANYONE HARM THEM HE SHALL BE SEVERELY PUNISHED.

RURU THEN WENT WITH THE KING TO THE PALACE, DISCOURSED TO THE QUEEN AND RETURNED TO THE FOREST.

the End.

THE HUNTER OUTWITTED

BROTHER, WILL YOU TEACH YOUR NEPHEW THE TRICKS OF OUR HERD?

CERTAINLY.

THERE ONCE LIVED A STAG IN THE FOREST NEAR RAJAGRIHA. ONE DAY HIS SISTER CAME TO HIM WITH HER SON.

GO HOME NOW, MY BOY, AND COME BACK TOMORROW.

NEXT DAY—

I WONDER WHAT UNCLE WILL TEACH ME.

EVERY DAY FOR TWO MONTHS THE LITTLE DEER WENT TO HIS UNCLE.

ONE DAY WHILE WANDERING THROUGH THE FOREST WITH HIS FRIENDS...

...HE STEPPED INTO A TRAP.

A..A..AH!

CLACK

HELP! I'M CAUGHT.

LET'S GO BACK AND TELL HIS MOTHER.

YOUR SON HAS BEEN CAUGHT IN A HUNTER'S TRAP.

OH DEAR, WHAT SHALL I DO?

SHE HURRIED TO THE STAG.

BROTHER, PLEASE HELP ME. MY SON HAS BEEN TRAP-PED.

DO NOT FEAR, MY SISTER.

I HAVE NOT TAUGHT HIM FOR NOTHING. HE WILL RETURN. HAVE PATIENCE.

MEANWHILE—

I MUST REMEMBER WHAT UNCLE TAUGHT ME.

*CAUTION PAYS

IN A FOREST NEAR VARANASI, THERE LIVED AN ANTELOPE WHICH WAS VERY FOND OF THE FRUITS OF A PARTICULAR TREE.

IN A VILLAGE NEAR BY LIVED A HUNTER, WHO KNEW THIS.

I MUST GET HIM TODAY.

EARLY THAT MORNING THE HUNTER WENT TO THE JUNGLE.

HMM. HE IS A BIG ANIMAL. I WILL GET QUITE SOME MONEY BY SELLING HIS MEAT.

HE PUT UP A *MACHAN ON THE TREE...

...AND WAITED FOR THE ANTELOPE.

HE SHOULD BE HERE ANY MOMENT.

* Based on Kurunga Jataka

* PLATFORM

AS USUAL THE ANTELOPE CAME STROLLING ALONG. MM..M..M. JUST THINKING OF THAT FRUIT MAKES ME HUNGRY.

HE WAS A CLEVER ANTELOPE AND NEVER MISSED A THING. HEY! A MAN'S FOOTPRINTS!

THERE MUST BE A HUNTER NEAR BY, WAITING TO KILL ME.

WHY DOESN'T HE COME NEAR? I SHALL TRY THROWING SOME FRUIT TO HIM. MAYBE THAT WILL LURE HIM TO THE TREE.

OH OH, THERE IS SOMEONE UP THE TREE. THE FRUIT IS BEING THROWN TO ME. IT ISN'T DROPPING AS IT USUALLY DOES.

YES. NOW I AM SURE. I CAN SEE THE CORNER OF A 'MACHAN'.

I'LL PRETEND TO TALK TO THE TREE AND SEE WHAT HAPPENS.

LISTEN, TREE. YOU HAVE ALWAYS DROPPED YOUR FRUIT ON THE EARTH. WHY DO YOU THROW IT AT ME TODAY?

HMMM. NO ANSWER. HE THINKS HE IS SMART, DOES HE?

AND SO TREE, SINCE YOU HAVE STOPPED BEHAVING LIKE A NORMAL TREE, I TOO WILL BEHAVE DIFFERENTLY. I SHALL EAT ELSEWHERE.

THE HUNTER KNEW HE HAD LOST HIS CHANCE AND THREW HIS JAVELIN AT THE ANTELOPE.

WOOOSH

HEE...HEE, TOO BAD, HUNTER! BETTER LUCK NEXT TIME.

THE GOLDEN ANTELOPE

POOR ANTELOPE! EVERY TIME HE SEES ME HE RUNS AWAY IN FRIGHT.

LONG AGO THERE LIVED A KING IN VARANASI WHO HAD A GARDENER NAMED SANJAYA. EVERY DAY AN ANTELOPE CAME TO GRAZE IN THE ROYAL GARDEN.

AFTER SOME TIME THE ANTELOPE BECAME ACCUSTOMED TO SEEING SANJAYA ABOUT AND STOPPED RUNNING AWAY.

ONE DAY WHILE HE WAS TAKING FRUIT AND FLOWERS TO THE PALACE, THE KING STOPPED HIM.

HAVE YOU NOTICED ANYTHING STRANGE IN THE GARDEN, SANJAYA?

NOTHING, YOUR MAJESTY, EXCEPT THAT A WILD ANTELOPE COMES TO GRAZE HERE FROM TIME TO TIME.

DO YOU THINK YOU COULD CATCH HIM?

OH YES. IF I HAD A LITTLE HONEY I WOULD BRING HIM RIGHT INTO YOUR PALACE.

* Based on Vatar Miga Jataka

24

THE KING ORDERED SOME HONEY TO BE GIVEN TO SANJAYA.

I SHALL COAT THE GRASS WHERE HE GRAZES WITH HONEY, THEN HIDE MYSELF AND SEE WHAT HAPPENS.

ALONG CAME THE ANTELOPE.

HMM. THIS GRASS TASTES EXCEPTIONALLY SWEET TODAY.

SO MY PLAN HAS WORKED. NOW FOR THE SECOND STAGE. HEE HEE.

THE ANTELOPE WAS SO SNARED BY THE TASTE OF THE SWEETENED GRASS, HE WOULD EAT NOWHERE ELSE.

HMM. NOW TO SHOW MYSELF GRADUALLY.

AT FIRST THE ANTELOPE WAS STARTLED AT THE APPEARANCE OF SANJAYA.

HUH?

BUT SOON HE WAS EATING THE SWEET GRASS THAT SANJAYA OFFERED HIM.

NOW I MUST LEAD HIM TOWARDS THE PALACE.

HE HASN'T EVEN NOTICED WE ARE NEAR THE PALACE.

ONCE HE WAS INSIDE THE PALACE, SANJAYA QUICKLY SHUT THE DOOR.

SLAM

AT THE SIGHT OF SO MANY MEN AND KNOWING THAT HE WAS TRAPPED, THE ANTELOPE BEGAN TREMBLING WITH FRIGHT AND DASHED TO AND FRO.

...

WHEN THE KING CAME DOWN FROM HIS CHAMBER AND SAW THE ANTELOPE HE FELT SORRY FOR IT.

ANTELOPES ARE SO TIMID THAT THEY NEVER REVISIT A PLACE FOR AT LEAST A WEEK IF THEY HAVE SEEN A MAN THERE.

SOMETIMES THEY NEVER GO BACK AGAIN. THIS ANTELOPE WAS CARRIED AWAY BY THE TASTE OF THE SWEETENED GRASS AND FORGOT HIMSELF.

SURELY THERE IS NOTHING VILER IN THE WORLD THAN THE LUST OF TASTE. YOU HAVE TAUGHT US A VALUABLE LESSON.

GO MY FRIEND. YOU ARE FREE TO GO WHEREVER YOU PLEASE.

*THE BANYAN DEER

IN TWO DIFFERENT PARTS OF A FOREST LIVED TWO HANDSOME GOLDEN STAGS. ONE WAS CALLED THE BANYAN DEER AND THE OTHER THE BRANCH DEER. EACH HAD A HERD OF ITS OWN.

NOW THE KING OF VARANASI WAS VERY FOND OF HUNTING DEER AND IN HIS LOVE OF IT HE DISTURBED ALL HIS TOWNSFOLK.

COME ON, EVERYONE, LET'S GO ON A HUNT.

ONE DAY THE PEOPLE GOT TOGETHER AND HIT UPON A PLAN.

LET US CHASE ALL THE DEER INTO THE KING'S GARDEN. THEN HE WILL NOT DISTURB US AT ODD HOURS TO GO INTO THE FOREST.

THEY GATHERED STICKS, POTS, PANS AND ANYTHING THAT MADE A NOISE TO DRIVE THE DEER INTO THE GARDEN.

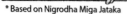

* Based on Nigrodha Miga Jataka

28

THE NEXT DAY THEY SURROUNDED THE FOREST AND CHASED ALL THE DEER INTO THE KING'S GARDEN.

THERE! NOW HE WILL NOT DISTURB US WITH SO MANY DEER SO NEAR HIM.

BANG CLANG

A FEW TOWNSMEN WENT TO THE KING

SIR, YOU DISTRACT US FROM WORK WHEN YOU GO HUNTING; SO WE HAVE DRIVEN ALL THE DEER INTO YOUR GARDEN. SHOOT THEM WHENEVER YOU WISH.

AND SO THE KING WOULD GO OUT AND SHOOT DEER NOW AND AGAIN.

I MUST WARN MY MEN TO LEAVE THE GOLDEN STAGS ALONE.

SOMETIMES THE HEAD COOK WOULD ACCOMPANY HIM ON HIS HUNT.

LOOK, MY LORD! THERE GOES A PLUMP ONE.

NOT HIM. HE IS A GOLDEN STAG.

BUT THE DEER WERE BEING SLAIN IN SUCH LARGE NUMBERS THAT THE BANYAN DEER DECIDED TO DO SOMETHING ABOUT IT.

MY FRIEND, OUR DEER CANNOT ESCAPE DEATH BUT LET THEM NOT BE KILLED NEEDLESSLY. WE WILL SEND THEM TO THE BLOCK BY TURNS—ONE FROM MY HERD ONE FROM YOURS— EACH DAY.

IN THIS WAY THE DEER WHOSE TURN IT WAS WOULD GO TO THE BLOCK AND WAIT UP FOR THE COOK TO TAKE HIM AWAY.

HMMM, THIS IS A NICE PLUMP ONE TODAY.

ONE DAY IT WAS THE LOT OF A DOE WHO WAS ABOUT TO BE A MOTHER. SHE WENT TO THE BRANCH DEER.

MY LORD, LET ME ESCAPE THIS TIME. WHEN I HAVE HAD MY LITTLE ONE THERE WILL BE TWO OF US TO GO TO THE BLOCK.

NO, NO, I CANNOT DO THIS. GO AWAY.

SO SHE WENT TO THE BANYAN DEER AND TOLD HIM HER STORY.

VERY WELL. YOU DON'T GO THIS TIME. I WILL DO SOMETHING ABOUT IT.

HE HIMSELF WENT TO THE BLOCK THAT DAY.

WHEN THE COOK CAME ALONG HE WAS SURPRISED TO SEE ONE OF THE GOLDEN DEER AT THE BLOCK.

OH, OH! I MUST TURN BACK AND TELL THE KING.

WHEN THE KING HEARD THE NEWS, HE WAS SURPRISED.

HE RUSHED TO THE SPOT.

WHY ARE YOU HERE? YOU ARE FREE TO LIVE.

YOUR MAJESTY, A DOE WHO WAS ABOUT TO BECOME A MOTHER CAME TO ME AND ASKED TO BE SPARED.

I HAVE COME IN HER PLACE. PLEASE SPARE HER.

THE KING WAS ASTOUNDED AT SUCH LOVE. HE WAS DEEPLY MOVED.

HE TURNED TO THE BANYAN DEER.

BOTH OF YOU SHALL LIVE. YOU DESERVE IT.

IF YOU CAN SPARE OUR LIVES, CAN'T YOU SPARE THE LIVES OF ALL THE DEER, YOUR MAJESTY?

I CAN! I WILL!

AND COULDN'T YOU SPARE THE LIVES OF ALL THE CREATURES IN YOUR FOREST, YOUR MAJESTY?

THE KING THOUGHT FOR A WHILE AND THEN—

ALL RIGHT! FROM THIS DAY, THERE SHALL BE NO HUNTING OR KILLING OF ANY KIND IN MY KINGDOM.

AND SO ALL THE ANIMALS IN THE FOREST LIVED IN PEACE AND HARMONY FOR A LONG TIME TO COME.